I0828565

Inside - Outside

Library of Congress Control Number: 2014915784

ISBN 10 - 0-9916630-5-5
ISBN:13 - 978-0-9916630-5-7

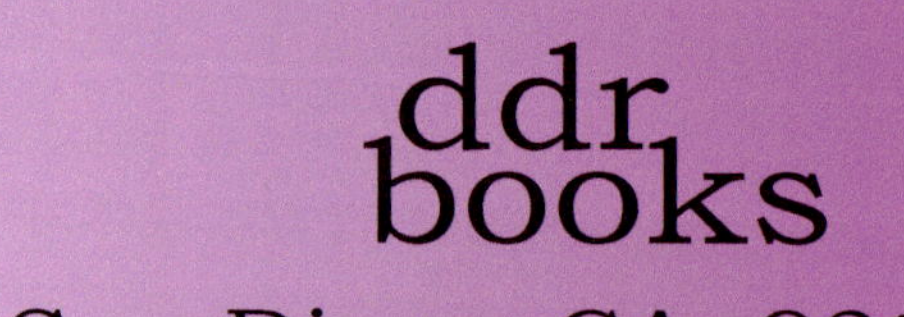

San Diego, CA 92119

Inside - Outside

D. D. Riessen

illustrated by:
Masaaki Kimura

To Kyo

It is to you

Mr. Death

that we march

with honor and glory,

blood and flames

to our early

yet eternally silent

graves.

Kazi was most happy when he was drawing. He drew people and flowers and buildings and bugs, most anything he could find.

His father was a machinist who worked with lathes and motors and all kinds of special tools to bend and cut and shape one thing into another.

Kazi watched for hours while drawing gears and spindles and springs and things.

"I will be an artist when I grow up.
Or, maybe an engineer."

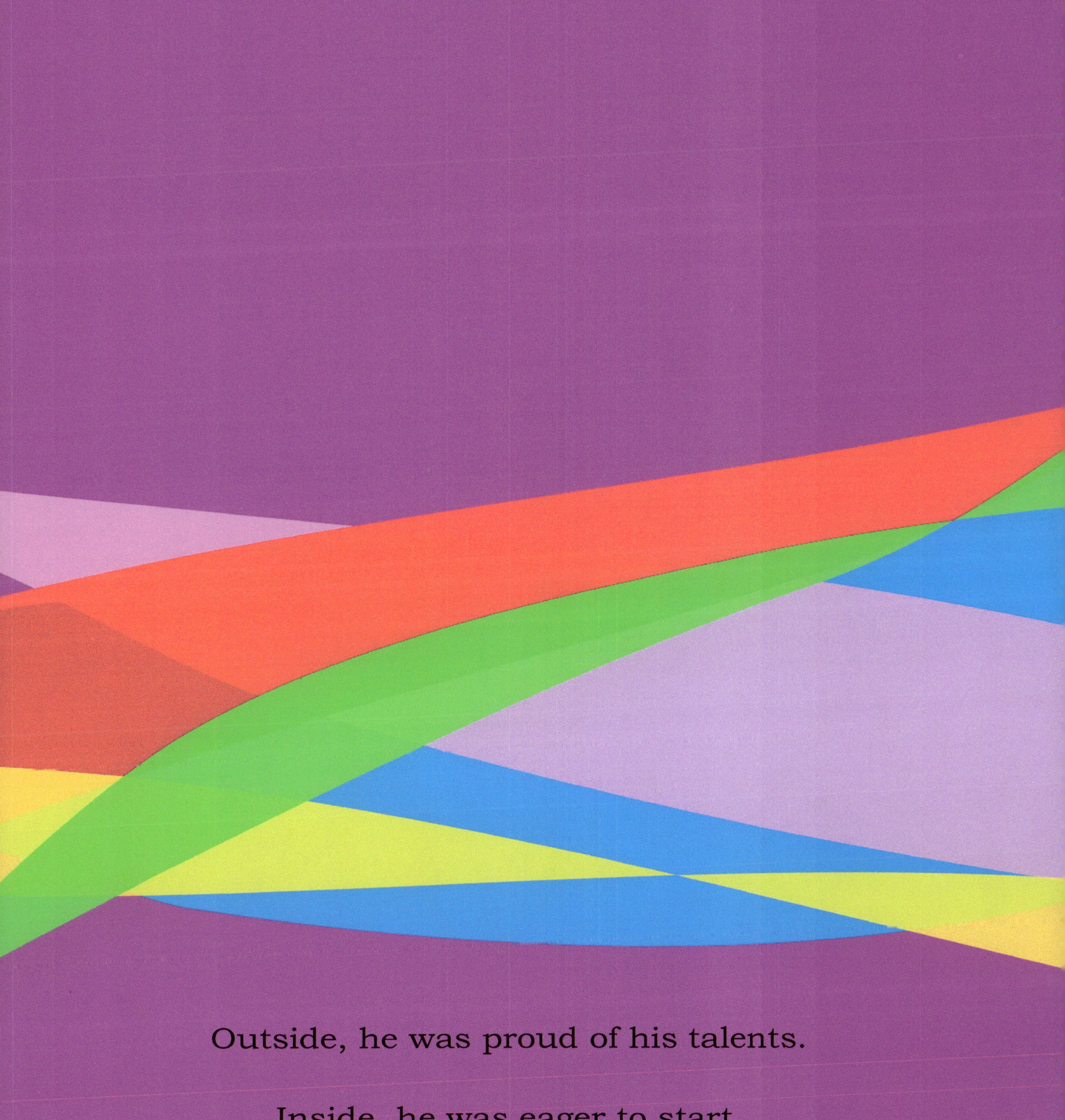

Outside, he was proud of his talents.

Inside, he was eager to start.

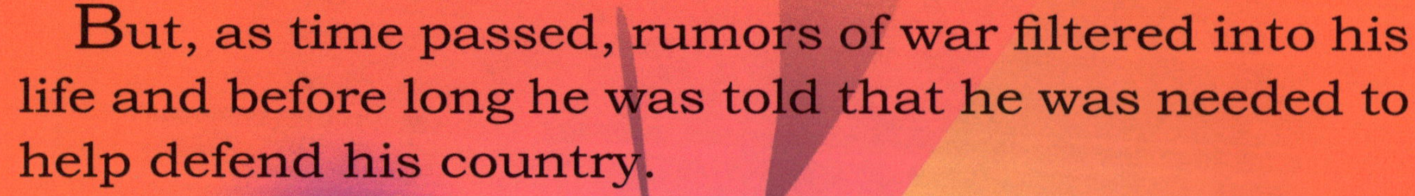

But, as time passed, rumors of war filtered into his life and before long he was told that he was needed to help defend his country.

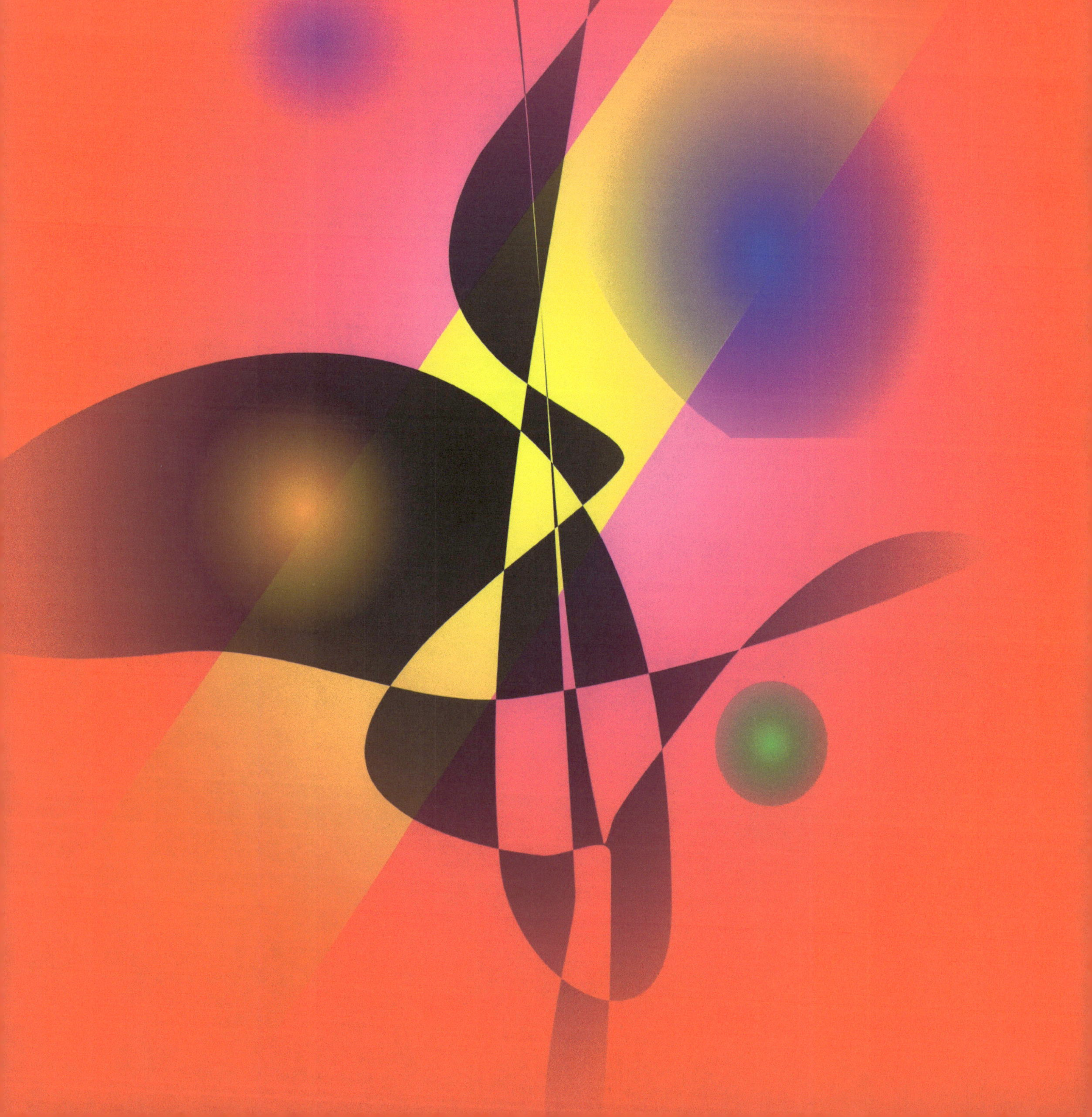

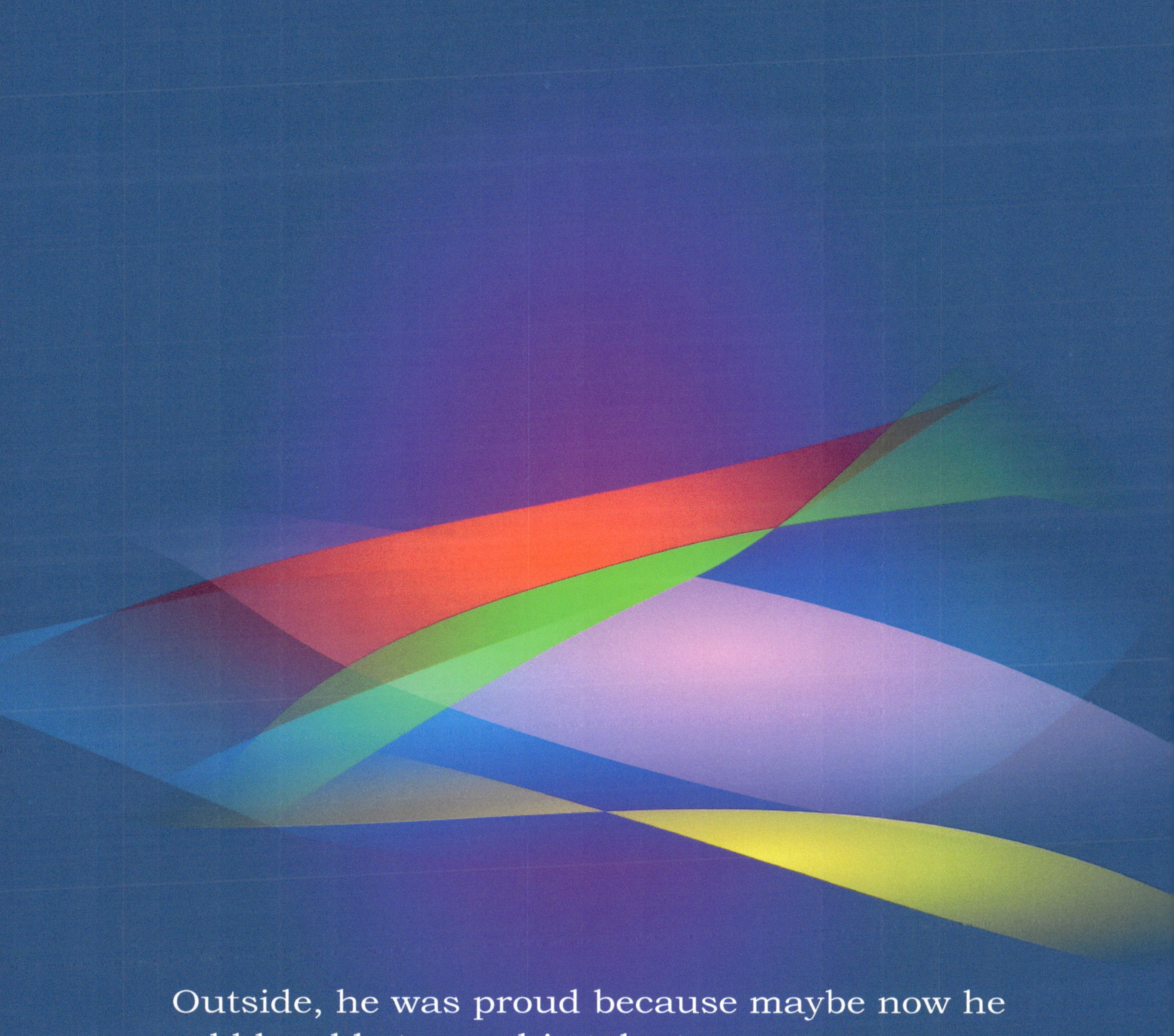

Outside, he was proud because maybe now he would be able to use his talents.

Inside, Kazi was happy to help.

But his country had other plans. "You will fly," he was told. "You will drop bombs on enemy targets and you will shoot these guns until you run out of bullets. And then you will crash your plane on top of them."

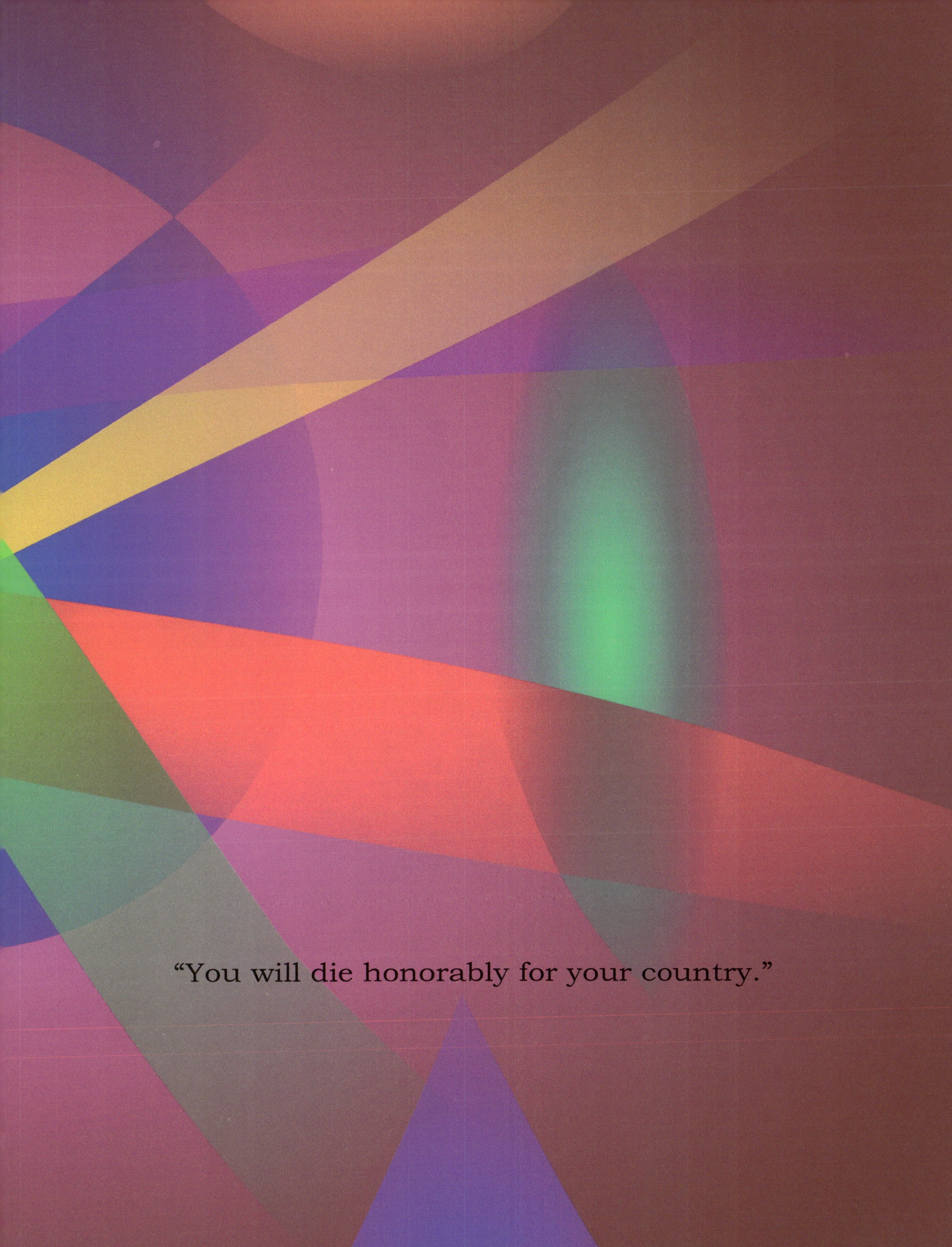
"You will die honorably for your country."

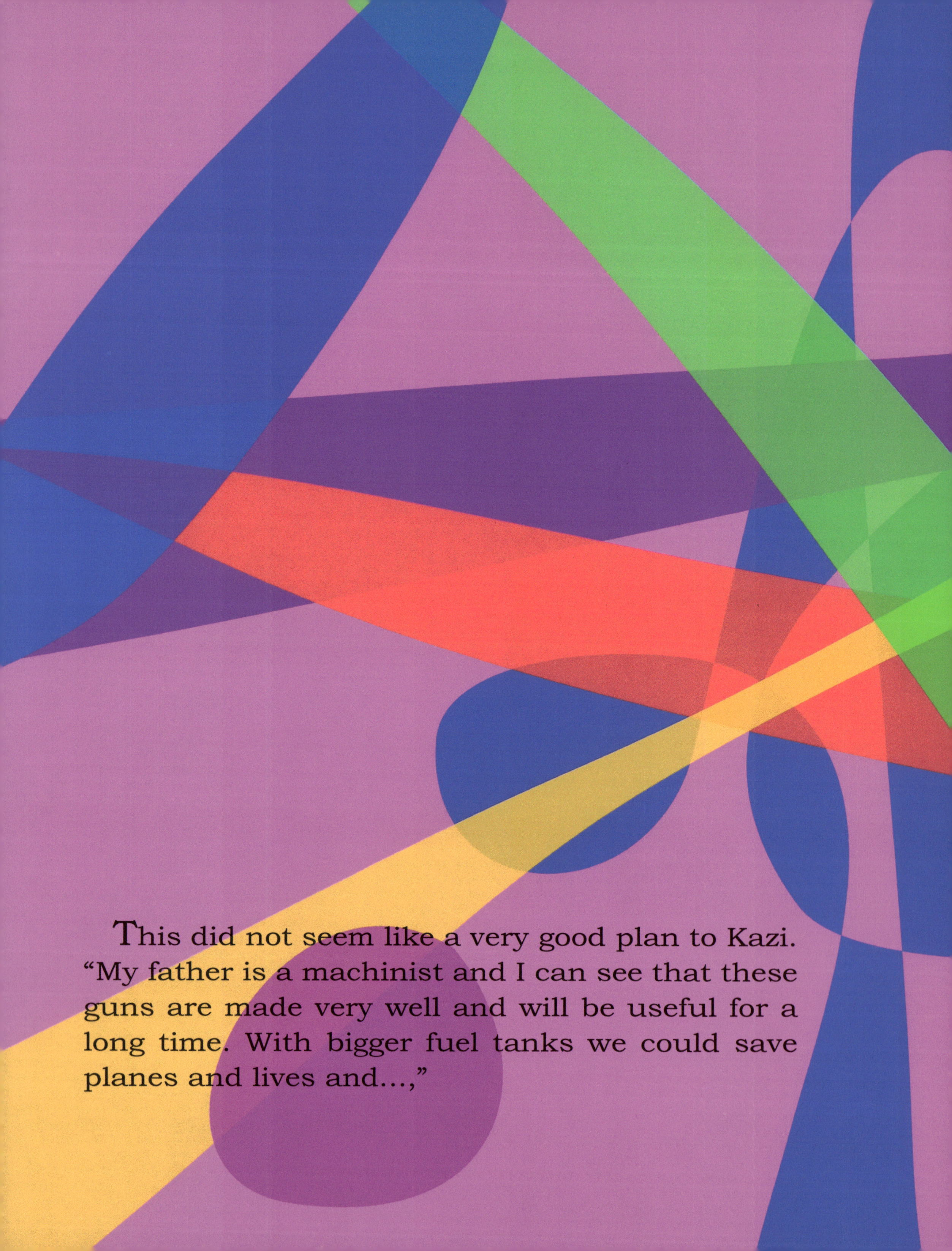

This did not seem like a very good plan to Kazi. “My father is a machinist and I can see that these guns are made very well and will be useful for a long time. With bigger fuel tanks we could save planes and lives and...,”

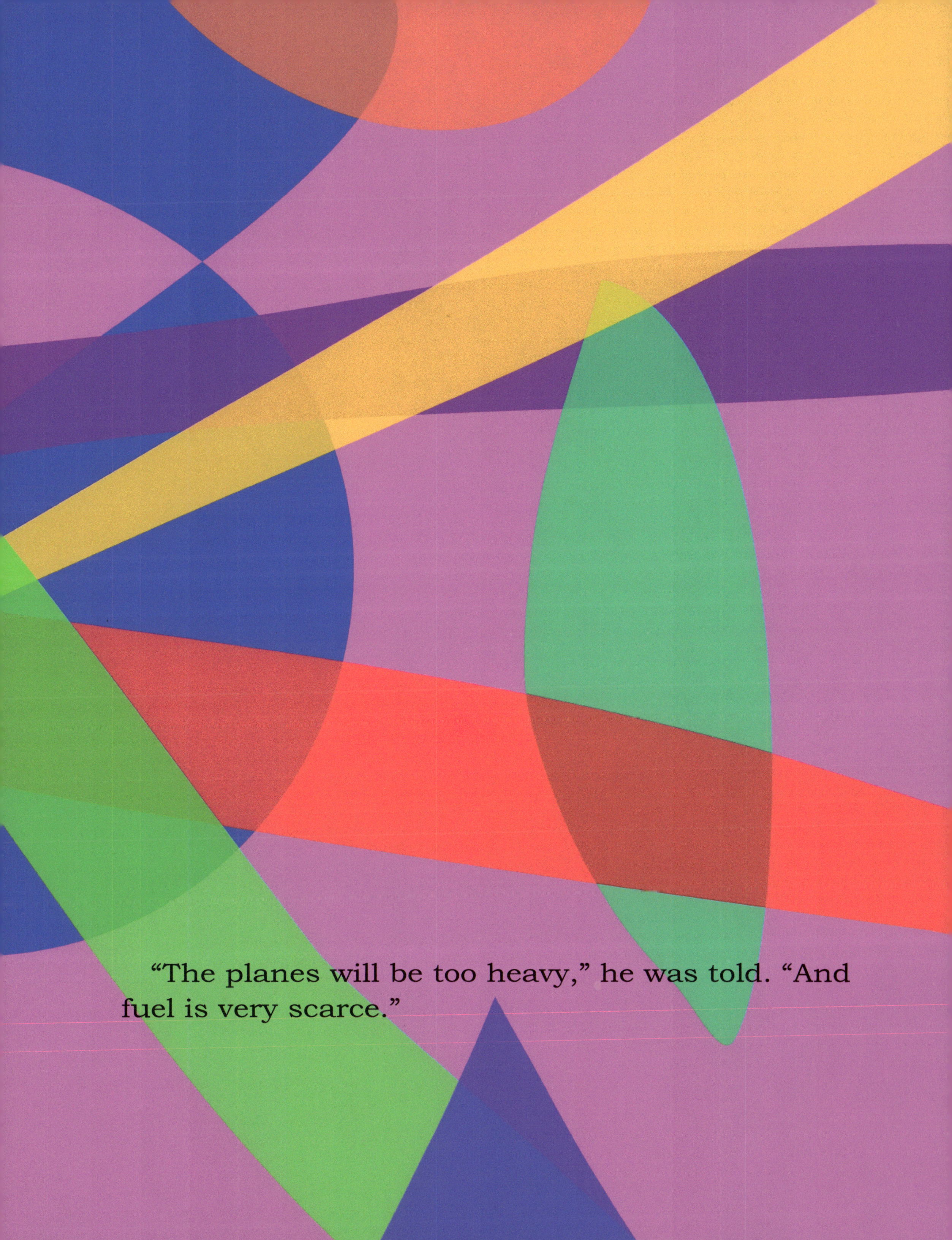

“The planes will be too heavy,” he was told. “And fuel is very scarce.”

Kazi was trained how to fly and how to kill.

Outside, he was proud to be part of the army that would help defend his country.

Inside, he thought he was sad but, after thinking about it, was surprised to discover that he felt nothing at all.

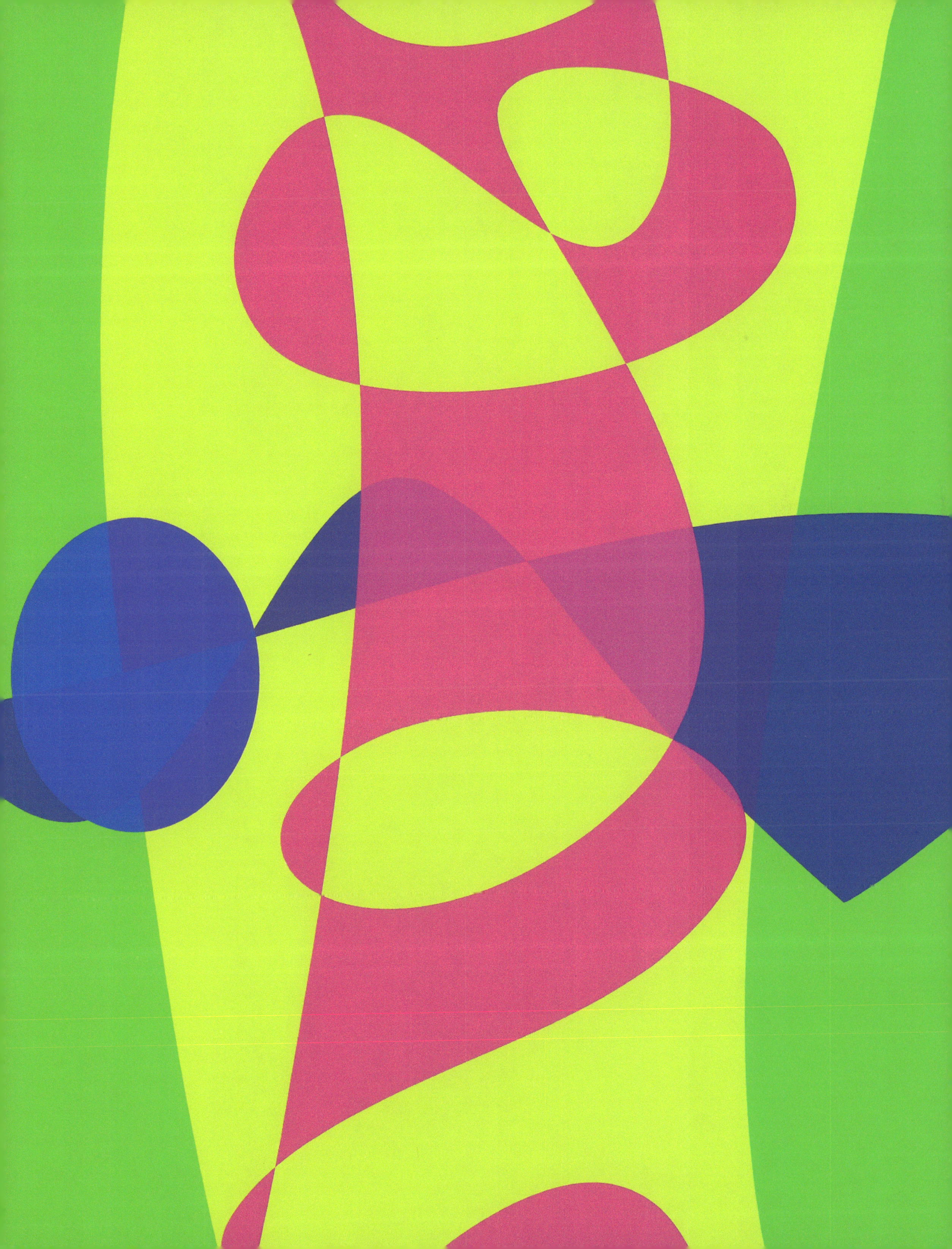

And then came the day that his orders arrived. Kazi's hands, so steady and skilled when he drew, were shaking as he opened the envelope to learn where his target would be and what would be the last day of his life.

Outside, he was brave.

Inside, he knew better than that.

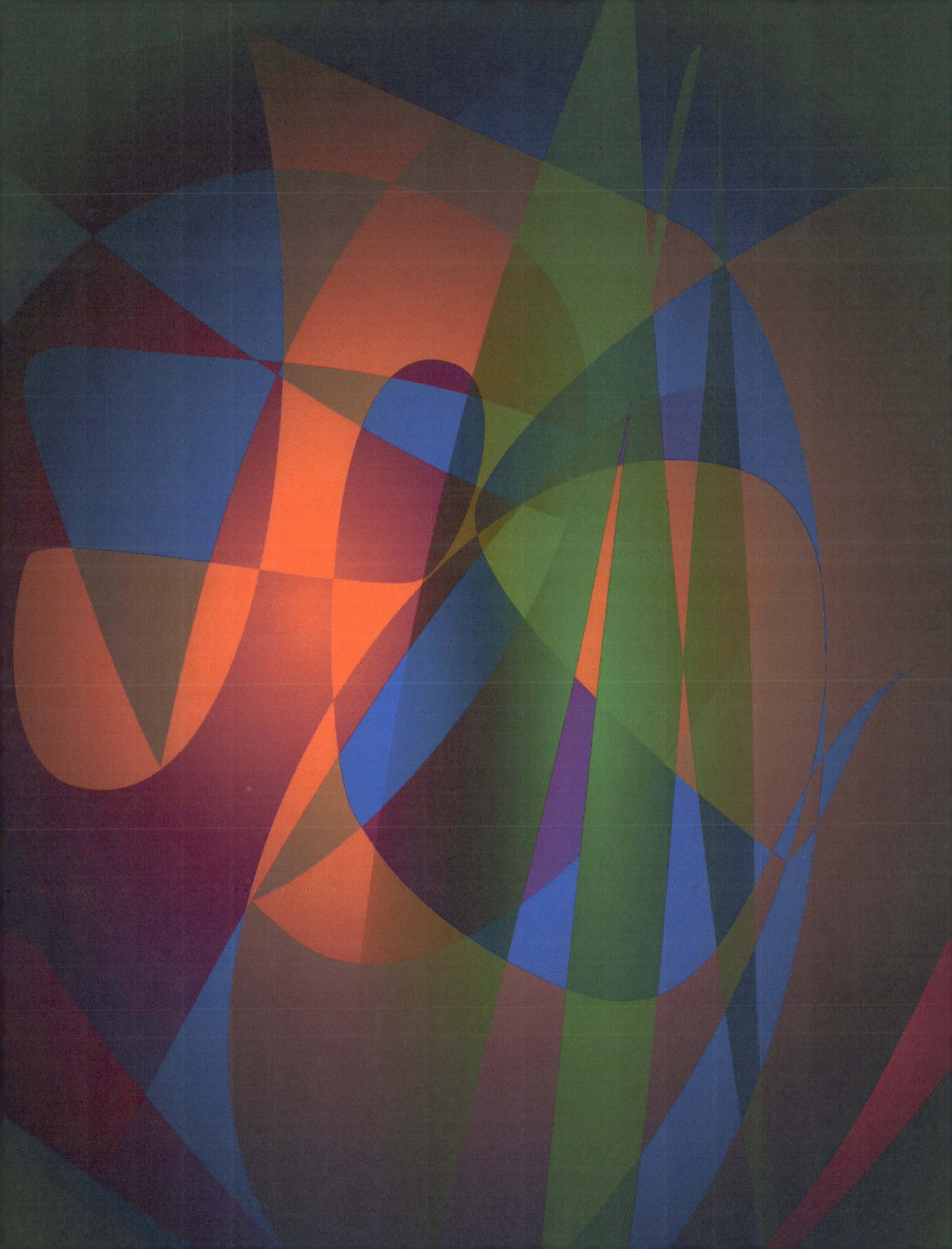

But Kazi learned that his country was short of planes and that his new task would be to swim up to enemy ships and blow a big hole in the side.

He would die honorably for his country.

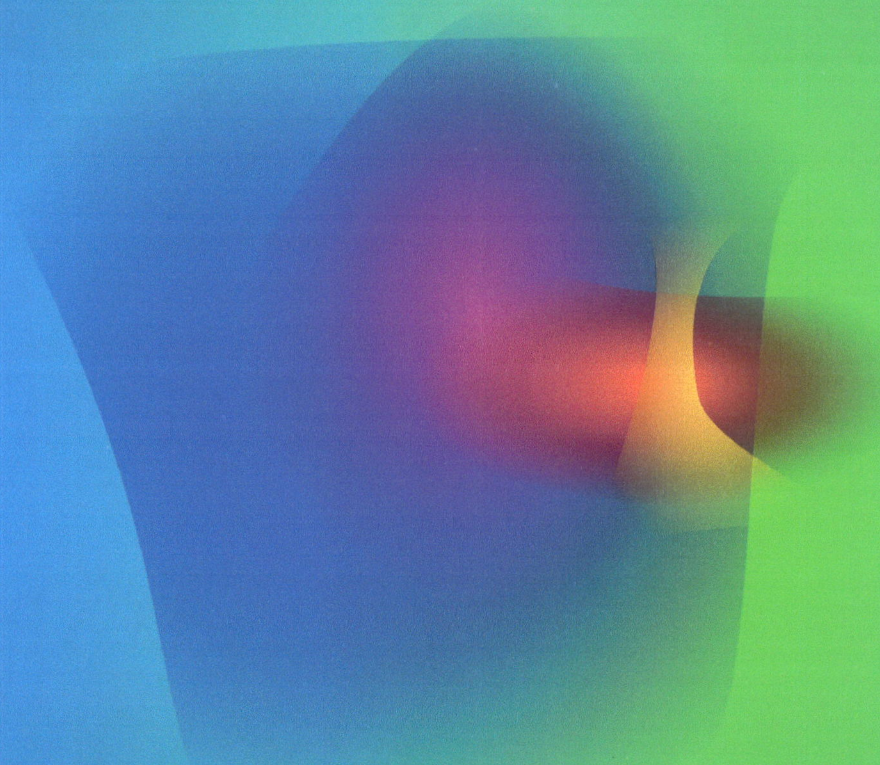

Outside, Kazi was loyal and brave. To defend his loved ones was the most important thing in the whole wide world.

Inside, he wondered if there might be a better way to solve all of these differences.

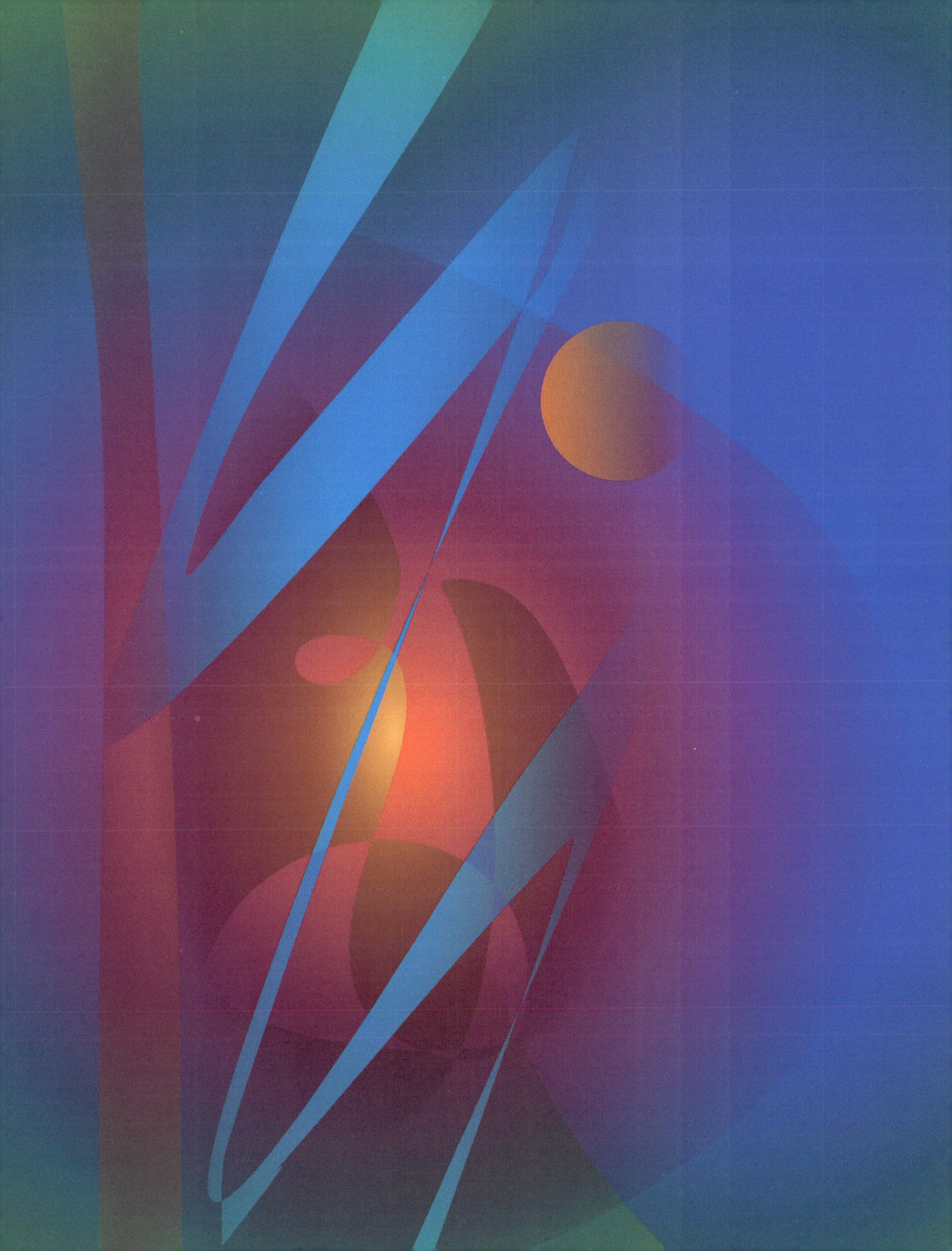

Kazi learned all about explosives and detonators and the most vulnerable parts of a ship. He was a good student because, thanks to his father, he understood design.

He would have been an engineer.

Outside, he was proud to be at the top of his class.

Inside, he knew that soon it wouldn't matter.

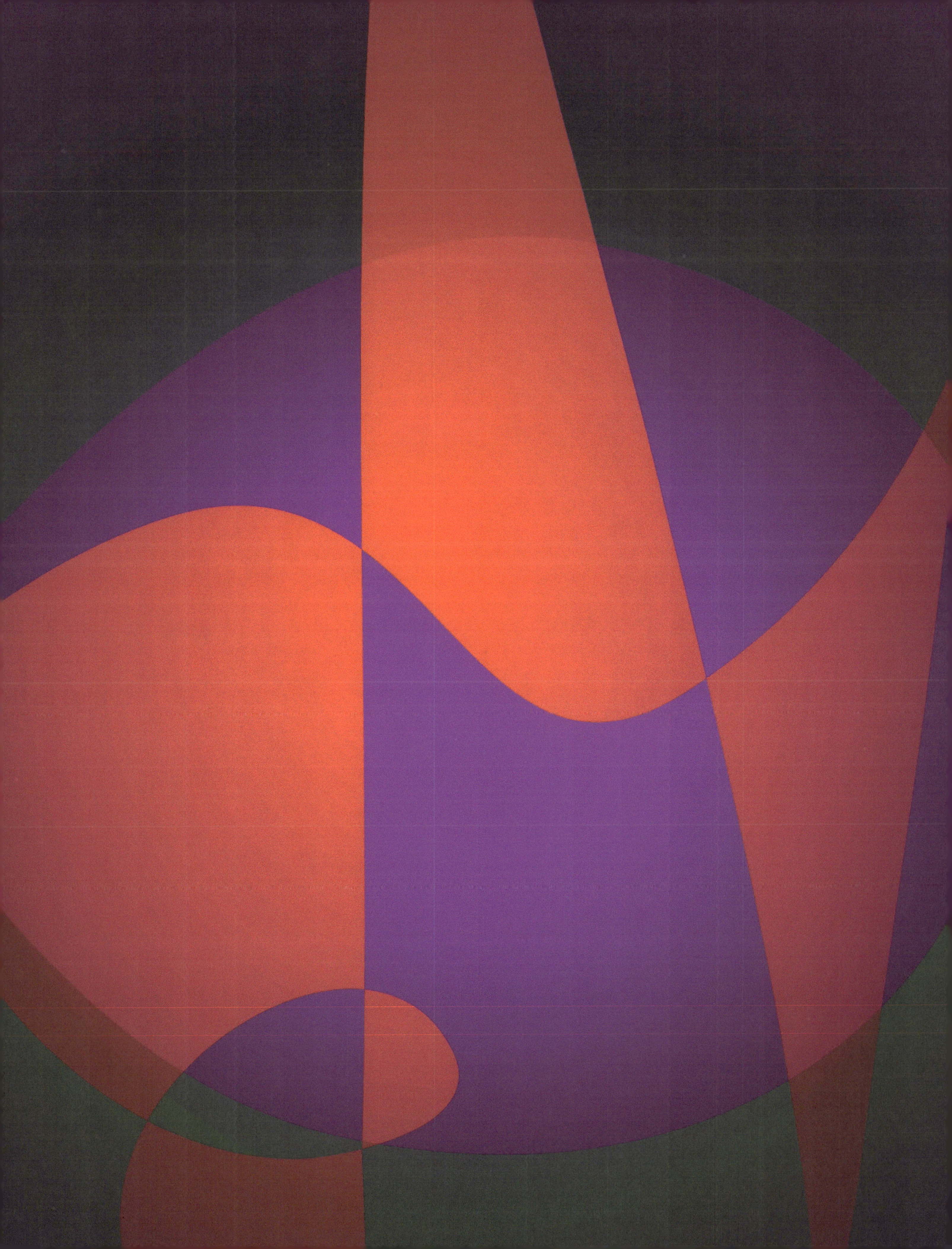

The war dragged on. There was much talk of victory, but always the news was murky. No one knew for sure.

Kazi knew his time was coming. Soon, it would be his turn.

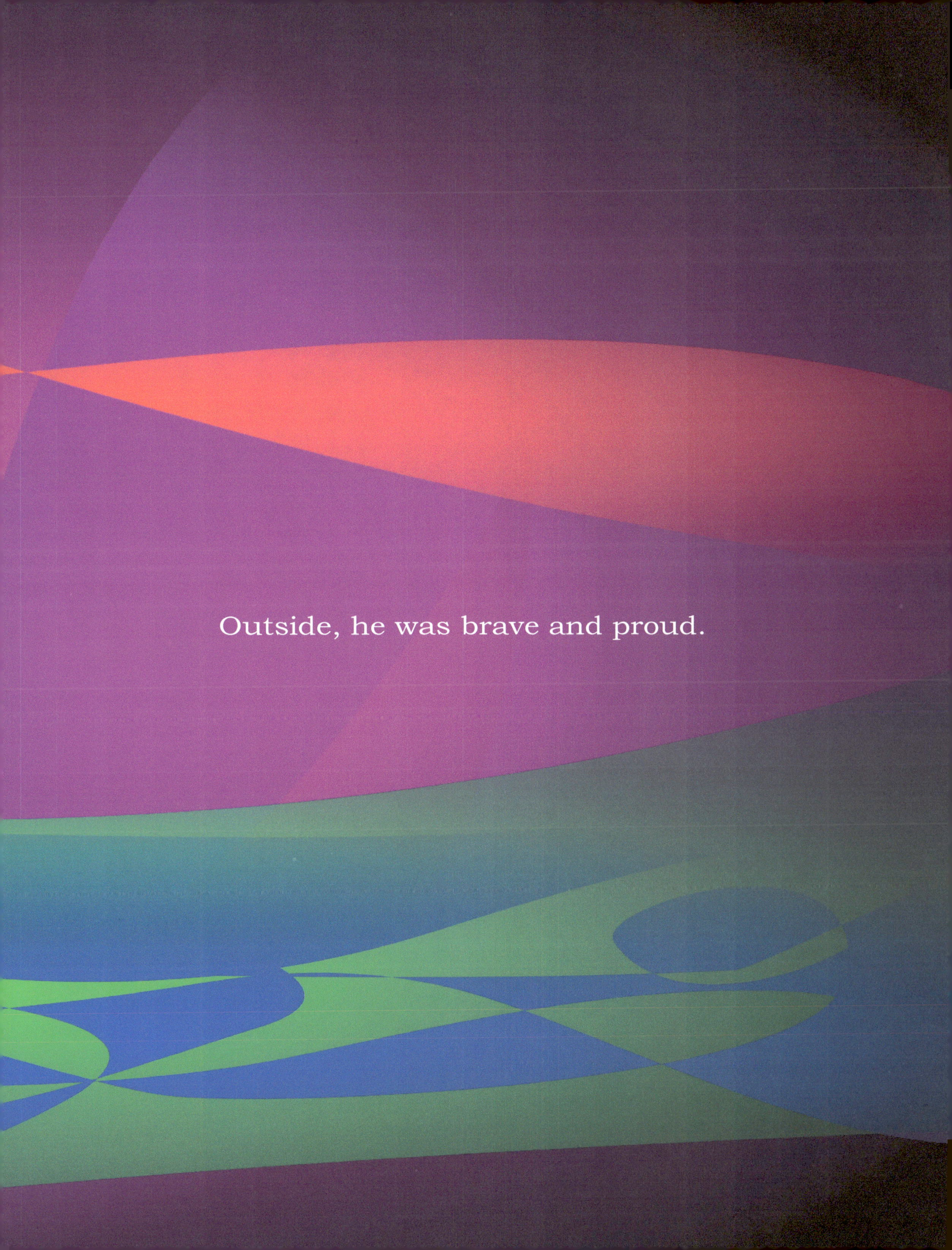

Outside, he was brave and proud.

There had been talk, rumors mostly, that the enemy had developed a very powerful bomb. Two of them had already been dropped on their cities.

The war was coming home. Kazi knew that his time was near.

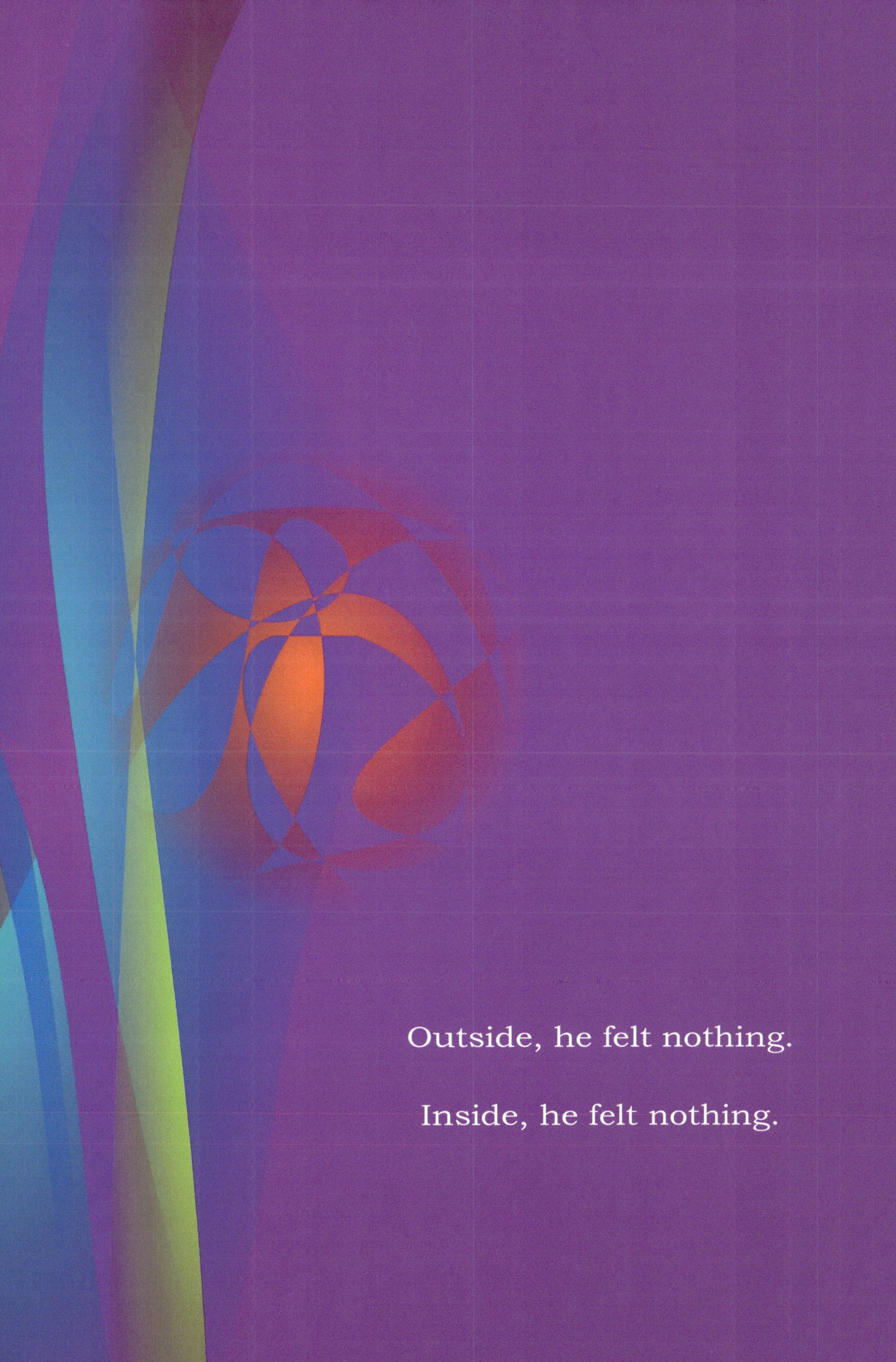

Outside, he felt nothing.

Inside, he felt nothing.

Soon after hearing about the bombs, Kazi was handed an envelope that would tell him where to go next and what to do when he got there.

He knew his life was over.

There would be no chance to be an engineer, an artist or an architect.

There would be no love of his life, no family, no children to love or to teach how to draw.

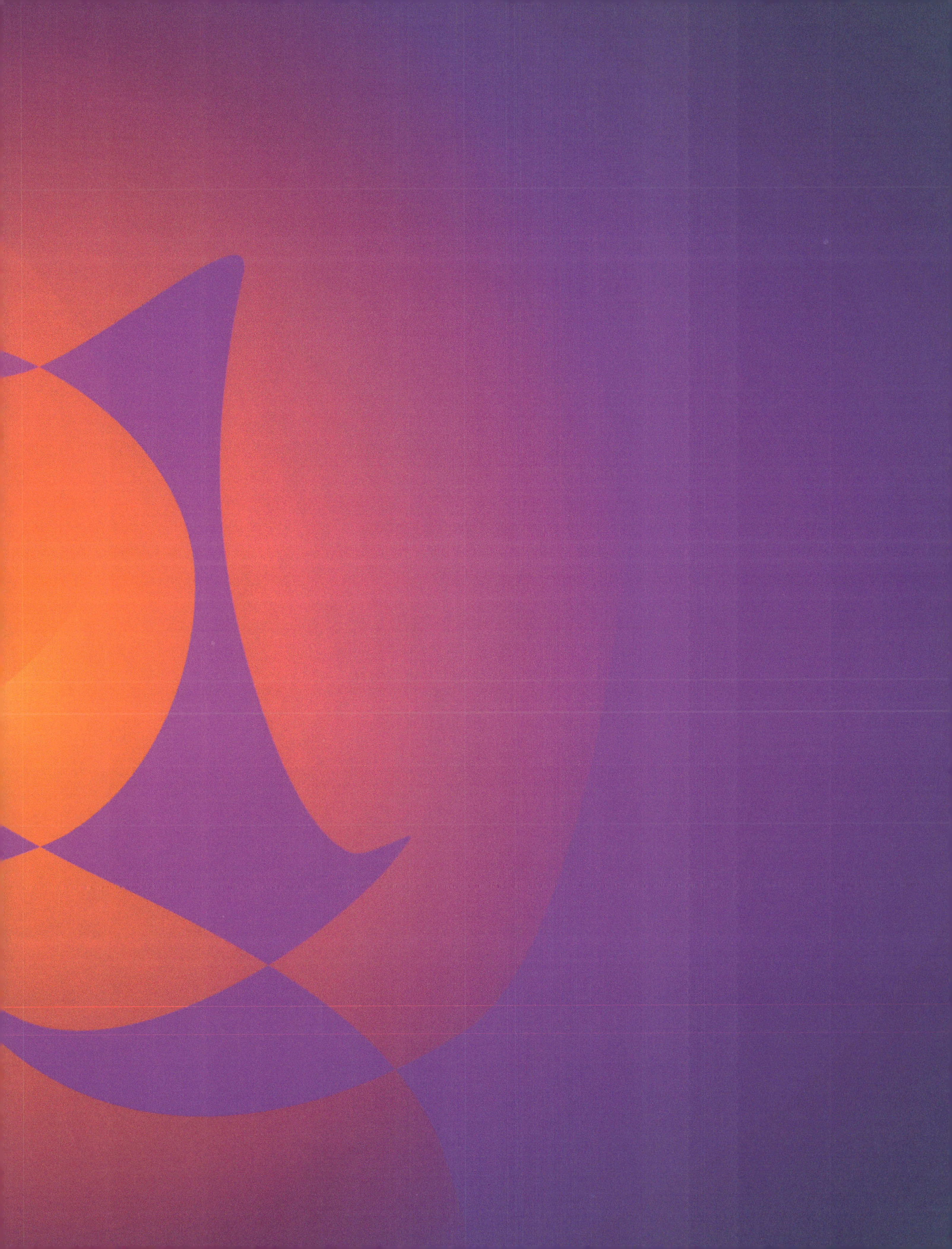

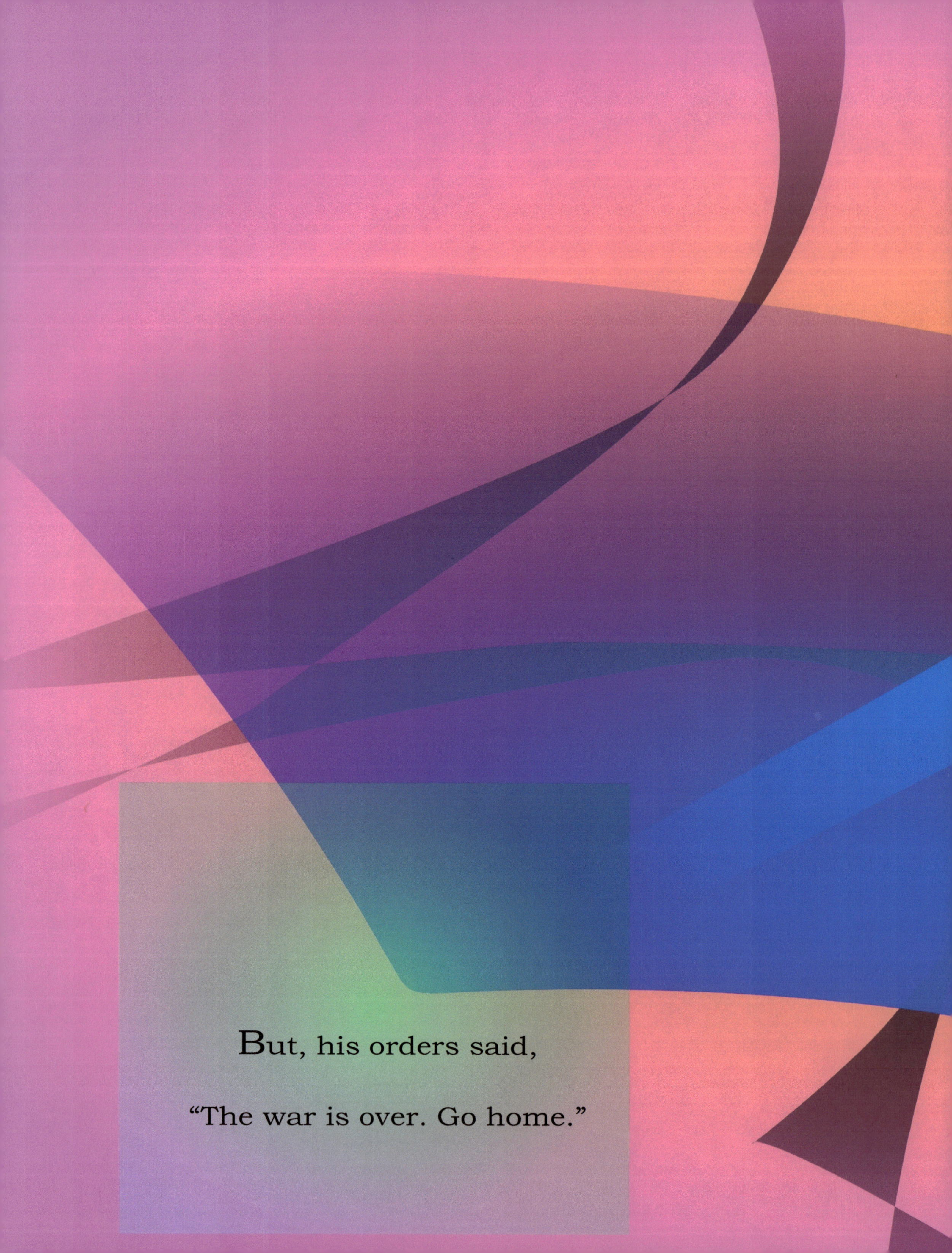

But, his orders said,

“The war is over. Go home.”

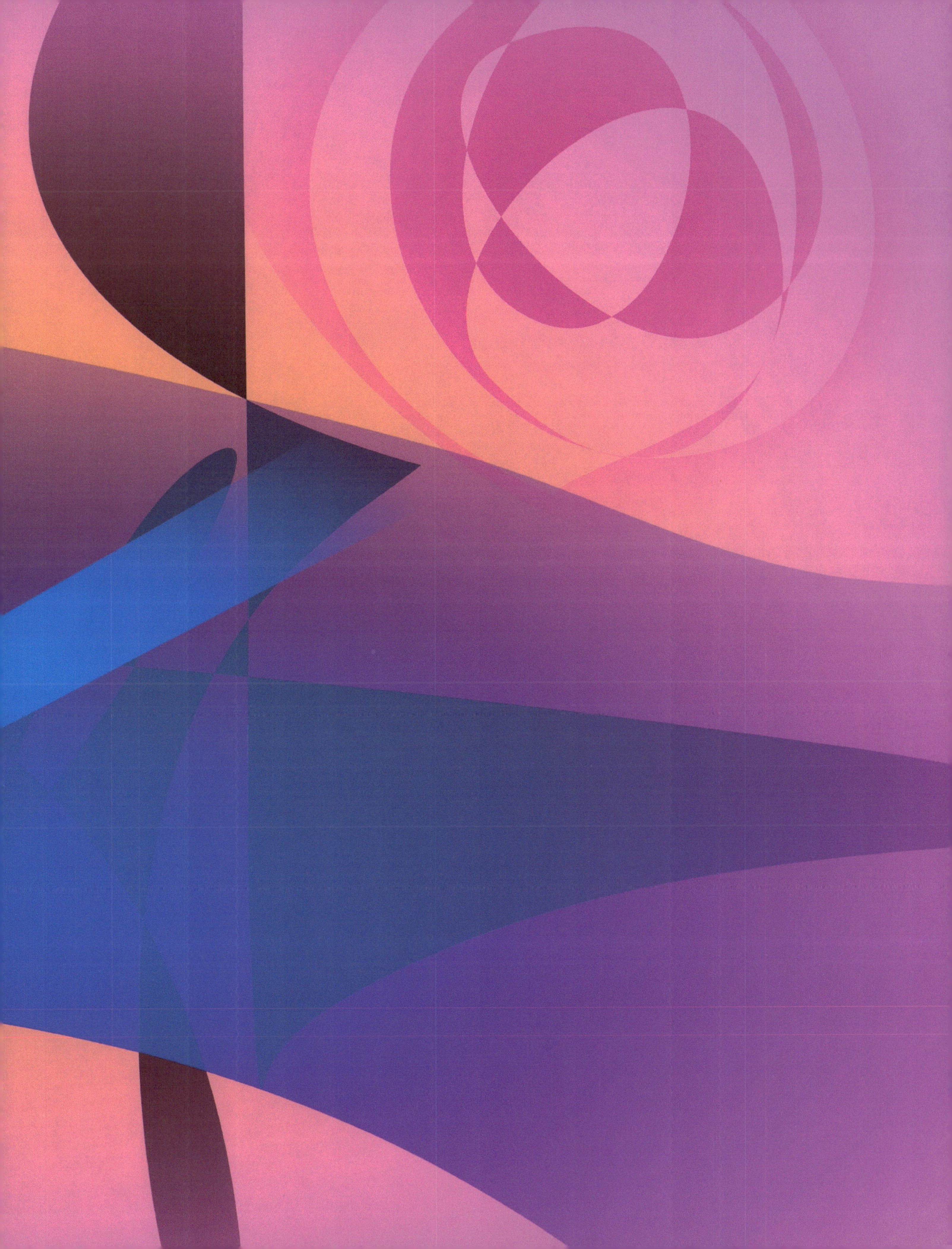

Carrying his bags, heading for the train station, Kazi listened to the children's laughter as they played in the streets, such a beautiful sound, so innocent and pure.

He walked by the houses and shops, saying hello to everyone, smelling what they were cooking and feeling like he was coming back to life.

For the first time in what seemed like an eternity, he noticed the flowers, intense greens, vibrant reds and oranges, brilliant colors under a stark blue sky.

Never had all of these things seemed so beautiful!

He found a place to sit and searched through his bags for his pencils. Soon, he was drawing flowers and buildings and bugs and people and clouds and even his own feet.

He drew everything he could see.

Outside, he was more than happy.

Inside, he was bursting with joy!

About the Author

Dave Riessen earned his Associate's Degree in Electronics at San Diego City College and then attended San Diego State University where he changed his major to English and focused on creative writing. He has written three novels:

You Gotta Have Wings (fiction, Nebraska,1954)
On Standby (adult fiction, California and Kansas,1990's)
Sometime Tomorrow (science fiction, Los Angeles, 2132)

Please visit my website at: www.ddriessen.com

About the Illustrator

Masaaki Kimura has been creating abstract art in Japan since 1970.

His major interest is happiness without cause, which he has been pursuing by means of visual art and poetry mixed with improvisational music.

www.ingramcontent.com/pod-product-compliance
Lightning Source LLC
LaVergne TN
LVHW070224110826
845147LV00003B/639

* 9 7 8 0 9 9 1 6 6 3 0 5 7 *